JUNIPER
Beyond the Veil

Sheesha Shapiro

Juniper

The Veil Awakening

Sheesha Shapiro

DEDICATION

My dearest friend, Lynn Frances

When you thought your world was crashing

I watched as your strength broke free

Spilling out to those around you

A gift you gave to me.

~ Chapter 1 ~

It was the screech of a hawk that woke him. As he laid there, he noticed a change in the air, and that's when the night came rushing back. She had tricked him, taking advantage of his desire, and now with the veil closed, how would he get back? And how much time had passed?

"I was wondering if you'd ever wake up."

Startled, Amias sat up to find an older gentleman sitting next to him. His long silver hair was tied back with a strap of leather. His sun kissed face was bearded and lined and his eyes so pale, one would think they were white.

The old man continued to look out into the sea, "From the looks of you, I'd say you've had one heck of a journey." Then, placing a blade of grass into his mouth, he turned to Amias, "If you are who I think you are, you're late."

Amias chose his words wisely, as to not give away too much information.

"I'm sorry, I must have fallen asleep. I'll gather myself and be on my way."

The old man grunted, "And where is "your" way guardian?"

Did he say guardian?

The old man stood up, brushing the sand off his linen pants and picking up his wooden staff, he began a slow stroll along the beach.

Turning back, "Are you coming or do you plan to sit there in the dunes?"

With hesitation, Amias rose and joined his new companion.

From the placement of the sun, he knew it was still early morning. In the distance several men were casting nets as seagulls dove in and out of the water around them. Still walking in silence, Amias's mind was swirling with questions. Where was he? How did this man know he was a guardian? How would he get back?

Offering Amias his flask, "I'm Rhen."

Amias recognized the contents of the flask. It was the same mead, made from fermented honey and water that he and his people drank. He hadn't realized how parched he was until he had an urge to finish it off.

Noticing Amias's reluctance, Rhen smiled, "Go ahead, and finish it. There is plenty more where that came from."

Emptying the flask he responded. "Thank you. I'm Amias."

Again, Rhen smiled. "I'm sure you have a lot of questions. But before you attempt to spin a tale of how you happened to be on my island, let me just say this, no one can just travel here. This island isn't on any map, it cannot be "found", understand?"

Amias nodded. "I'm really not sure where to begin. The last thing I remember was that I had ingested something that put me in a drunk like state. I must have passed out. Then I woke up here."

 Rhen just nodded his head as he directed their walk away from the beach and into a small village of cobblestone and whitewashed buildings. Amias noticed that like his own realm, this village too had no modern electricity. There was no hum of telephone lines, and the air was clean of pollutants.   Confirming he did not go through the right veil.

Pointing to a two-story shop with his staff, "Let's get some food and drink in our bellies. From the sounds coming from your gut, you could use it".

Then, with a slap on his back Amias was led over the threshold and into his own awakening.

~ Chapter 2 ~

The white washed room was dimly lit with lanterns. A stone fireplace roared, bouncing the reflection of a cat that sat among the piles of books scattered along a large wooden table. Amias watched as Rhen settled himself down in one of the overstuffed chairs near the fireplace.

There was something familiar about how the old man held himself, yet he couldn't quite place it. As he took the other chair across from him, Amias could hear the clanking of dishes. His stomach began to rumble as the aroma of sweet breads, eggs, and coffee filled the air.

A woman's voice broke the silence. "How was your morning walk Uncle? Did you snare anything?"

Rhen let out a deep chuckle, "Oh I snared something", giving Amias a wink.

It was as if she just magically appeared. He never heard her footsteps or felt the air move when she passed him, but there she was, standing with her back towards him as Rhen removed a plate and cup from the tray she was holding.

"You really need to start dressing in warmer clothing," she scolded. "I, nor you can hold off the coming winter."

"I know, I know." Rhen grumbled between bites. "This is Amias, the fashionably late guardian."

The woman turned to greet him. Is this a joke? A game? Amais mouth gaped, "Rowan?"

"Wrong tree." Extending the tray to him, "I'm Juniper."

Abruptly, Amias stood and started pacing the plank floor, breaking the stillness.

"What kind of sick game are the two of you playing?"

"Game? What on earth are you implying dear boy?" Rhens voice had turned firm from the accusation.

"This! She! She is Rowan!" Amias shouted. "And you sir...I have yet to place, but I'm sure Keelen has put you up to this."

Juniper placed the tray she had been holding during Amias's outburst on the table. Scooping up the cat and settling in the chair that was earlier occupied by him, "I'm not sure if I should be insulted or flattered, but I can say I am intrigued. Who are these people you speak of? And why the suspicion?"

Rhen rose and offered his chair to Amias. Then poured himself another cup of coffee before pulling up another chair.

Juniper watched as Amias rubbed his hands up and down his thighs nervously. Her curiosity of him was mixed with an unwanted desire to comfort. She knew it was dangerous for her to have emotions, especially ones that crept up from nowhere.

Those were the hardest to tame. Those were the ones that could cause destruction.

Rhen reached into his pocket and pulled out a pipe and began to fill it. He could see the objection on Amias's face.

"Don't worry guardian, this is not tobacco, it's an herb. I have a feeling there are many roads in your story, and although I do not know you personally, I can assume whatever path you chose, you did it for very good reasons." And with that, he began to smoke his pipe, filling the air with a waif of mint and cherry.

Exhaling, he continued, "The reason I seem familiar to you is because Vardon is my brother and Juniper is his daughter, and your charge."

Amias looked over at Juniper who was now circling her finger over her coffee as her spoon stirred it. She must have sensed him watching her, because as she slowly lifted her eyes to meet his, she smirked. The similarity was confusing him and the urge to explore her, a battle.

Amias's voice cracked, "Rhen, please don't take this wrong, but Juniper is not Vardon's daughter, Rowan is. And, I would know because I have been watching over her since her awakening."

"Let me get this straight, are you telling me that you already have a charge? And that charge looks identical to Juniper?" questioned Rhen.

Juniper had now swung her legs over the arm of the cushioned chair. Amias noticed that several buttons on her navy skirt had come undone, drawing his eyes to the bare skin above her knee high boots. She could feel his stare on her naked skin, and without thinking she began to slowly run her finger under her socks...lingering, making him want her.

Meeting his eyes with hers, "If this is true, then the Gods have a bigger plan or a sick sense of humor."

Rhen began laughing, "Ah yes, the Gods. If there are two of them, you have your hands full."

Juniper stood up, placing the sleeping cat on Rhen's lap, then grabbing her hooded cloak, she started for the door. "I'm finding all this mystery a bit annoying. I'm heading home".

Rhen re-filled his pipe, and without looking up, "Take Amias with you, and go slow, he's not used to your type of power."

Juniper knew not to question her uncle. She was sure he had a perfectly good reason for throwing him into her space and not asking more questions. She hated when he would let things ferment.

"Fine. Come on guardian, you could use a bath and a haircut."

Amias was confused, "Rhen are you sure it's a good idea for me to go? And to be alone with her?"

Standing up, "I'm not worried about her, it's you that may be in trouble," and with that said, Rhen winked and tossed Amias a coat.

****

Amias kept his hands in the coat pockets as he followed Juniper down the cobblestone street. It was the only thing he could think of doing to keep himself from reaching out and touching her.

As they made their way through town, he noticed something odd. The few townspeople that were walking about, would smile in their direction, yet immediately cross the street. He didn't think Juniper even noticed them. From the expressions crossing her face, it appeared she was having a conversation with herself.

"There," she pointed. "At the Northernmost point of the island. That's where we are heading."

Jutting out from the shoreline was a strip of land that connected to another land mass to which a cottage with a lighthouse stood. Its white tower, though worn from years, maybe centuries of harsh weather, stood strong, as it's black lantern room continued to be the glimmer of hope for those at sea. Flanked on either side, at least 15 feet high, stood two beautiful trees. Its branches twisted around one another, reaching upward like outstretched hands.   And as they approached, Amias could see that the branches were adorned with different shaped stones that hung from leather straps, ribbon and twine.

Holding one in his hand, "What are these? And these trees...they're majestic."

Juniper smiled, but not at Amias. She smiled at her trees.

 "I see I have my work cut out for me. For a man that comes from so much knowledge, you know so little."

"It's not that I know so little, it's that I was only schooled on what was necessary", Amias said in defense of his questions.

Touching several stones, Juniper began with his first lesson.

"These stones are called holey stones or witch stones." Pulling one out of her cloak pocket, Juniper carefully placed it in Amias's hand so as to not touch him.

"The holes in them are created by the sea. They are thought to be a powerful talisman, and it is said that if one breaks that the power inside them was used up protecting a life." This time, smiling at him, she peered through another, "And, if you are lucky enough, you can see the Fae."

Walking to the door, Juniper looked over her shoulder at Amias, "As for the trees, they are Juniperus chinensis, or hollywood juniper." And with that, she disappeared inside.

Amias smiled to himself pocketing the talisman.

~ Chapter 3 ~

Juniper was already in the tiny kitchen starting a fire in the potbelly stove when Amias entered her haven. All around him were books. Piles and piles of books. The wall that separated the large main room from the kitchen was a giant bookcase that had an attached ladder with rollers so one could reach one of the thousands of adventures. He watched her through a doorway of the bookcase. The way she moved struck him with curiosity, it was if she was floating above the stone floor. The more he watched, the more he saw the differences. Yes, he thought, she does look like Rowan, but he could see something more, something fragile yet strong in her demeanor. She was her own person.

Placing a kettle on top of the stove, Juniper looked out into the living area, "Could you make yourself useful and start a fire in the fireplace? I'm heating up water so you can bathe." Then pointed to the brass tub that sat in front of it before turning back around.

Amias lit the kindling and within minutes the fire was roaring. He noticed there wasn't much furniture. There were no silks or satins like the castle or sanctuary. A large hammock hung in the left corner of the bookcase, an area rug underneath, a lantern hung overhead, and more piles of books. He wandered around the room, touching the loom and spinning wheel. He unopened jars from a cabinet and smelled their contents. When Juniper finally joined him, Amias was standing in front of her bed.

She wanted to say don't even think about it, it's never going to happen, but she couldn't lie to herself.

Instead, she flashed a pair of scissors, "I think it's time to cut those knots out of your hair. Come sit over here." She then pulled up a stool next to the tub and patted the seat.

"I don't know about cutting all my hair off," Amias said as he walked over and took a seat.

"Have you looked at yourself?" Juniper handed Amias a mirror and waited for his response.

Amias couldn't believe what he saw. His once long plaited hair was now a mass of dreadlocks with pieces of sea grass tangled in, his skin was ashy and dry, and his full lips had become chapped from dehydration. No wonder, he thought. No wonder he wasn't able to turn her eye in his direction, he was beyond disheveled.

"I normally don't look like this," he said as he handed her back the mirror.

"Considering that you were late arriving here, I'm going to assume you went through a lot before the veil re-opened," Juniper replied as she began to snip. "Did you know that we hold energy and our past within the strands of our hair? So...consider this a much needed re-birth. If you are to take me on as your charge, you must let go of your past and past indiscretions. A clean slate."

Juniper continued to remove Amias's locks, tossing his hair into a basket, and trying not to brush against him as she circled around his body. When she reached the back of his head and made one last snip, her eyes grew big. There, on the back of Amais's neck was a birthmark in the shape of a crescent. Without thinking and without hesitation, she touched it. It shimmered as soon as her fingertips met his skin.

"OUCH!" yelped Amias as he leapt off the chair.

"What did you just shock me with?"

Letting out a sigh, "me", she said. "It was me touching you that shocked you."

Juniper began pouring the hot water into the tub, "I'm going to find you some clean nightwear. I'm sure Rhen left some here before he moved into town. The soap is in the cheese cloth on the tray under the tub."

And with that said, Juniper opened a large wooden door and began climbing the staircase, leading her up into the tower.

The hot water felt good as it warmed his sore muscles. He hadn't realized how achy and tired he was until he laid back, his body sinking deeper into the water, his eyes growing heavy. He could smell the chamomile and lavender soap through the cheese cloth and he pondered the idea of staying and not returning to his realm.

Juniper stood at the bottom of the stairs and watched him. She watched as the man that once looked like a nomad, materialized into a god-like creature. His now short cropped hair allowed his strong jaw-line and high cheekbones to emerge. If only she could touch him, she thought. To read him with her finger-tips, like one of her books. The fire bounced off the water, radiating an aura around him. His skin reminded her of caramel, creating a static charge throughout her body.

She ran her tongue across her lip, "How's the water? Getting cold yet?"

Again, he never heard her coming. There was no shift in the air or a shuffling sound of her feet, yet there she was, standing beside the basin. He quickly grabbed a cloth to cover himself.

"How do you do that?"

"Do what?"

"Not make a sound when you enter a room? And it's not just the no sound thing. It's as if your feet never touch the ground, as though you're hovering or floating."

Juniper brushed a strand of hair out of her eyes as she knelt down beside the tub.

"Did you know that some immortals choose the winds as their earthly bodies?"

Amias wasn't sure if she was just making a statement or implying something.

"Let me show you something," she continued.

Amias watched as Juniper held her small hands over the tub of water. Her fingers moved in circular motions, and in moments, the water began to move with them. Just like the spoon earlier at Rhen's.

"Now...let me warm up your bath" Juniper started to immerse her hands into the water.

"Wait!" Amias cautioned. "The one time you touched me, it wasn't a nice experience. Are you trying to electrocute me?"

"I'm sorry about that. I didn't mean to. And just so you know, I don't always "shock" those I touch or those who touch me back. It's just that there needs to be permission. I'll explain more lately. Now, time to warm up this water."

He couldn't figure out how she was doing it. At first it was a small vibration, then a warmth of small bubbles appeared as she remained focused. Her fingertips brushed his thigh and he no longer felt the need to remain covered. And, once again, with the skill of her hands, the water was warm.

Before he came to be in her presence, he would have been reserved, cautious with his words and actions, but now, he felt embolden just by the strength she emitted. Yes, he thought, yes, he was attracted to Rowen, but not like this. Perhaps the hunger he once felt for her had nothing to do with her at all. Perhaps it had everything to do with his own need to control and have what was not his. And now, the desire to "control" and "have" had been replaced with a hunger to be hers. Taking the chance of being painfully shocked, Amias sat forward, reached out with both hands and pulled Juniper into the tub of water, sliding her body on top of his. There was no resistance from her when his mouth met hers, instead he felt the sweetness of her tongue. And when his hands began to explore underneath her wet gown, Juniper sat up, still straddling his body, removed her clothes.

"Took you long enough. I thought for sure we were going to play some cat and mouse game forever, and this tigress needs a lion not a mouse."

Amias smiled as she gave him permission to enjoy her.

Juniper could tell that Amias was still unsure on how to proceed. Another lesson, at another time, she thought. Focusing on bringing out this beautiful man's unbridled passion, she skillfully began exploring his muscular torso, leaving kisses as she moved her way down between his strong thighs.

His moans escaped him without hesitation, as he watched Juniper command every movement, every sensation, with the circular motion of her tongue, and the ardor in her lips. Was it because it had been so long? Or was it skill? Amias had little time to think. With his hands grasping at the edge of the tub, her hands cupping his ass, Amias peeked with a pulsating burst of elation.

Juniper's first step in enchantment was short-lived. Her attention now was drawn towards the sound of the shutters banging to the chorus of the rain.

Juniper stepped out of the tub, she could hear that a storm was raging outside. She wanted to continue to stand there, in the firelight, allowing Amias to resume adoring her, but there was a bigger matter to take care of. Fearing the clashing of the sky had everything to do with her and not Mother Nature, she grabbed her long cardigan sweater and her leg-warmers and started for the tower.

Amias watched as she scurried around the room. He wished she would stand still so he could take delight in her nakedness. The curve of her hips, the power in her thighs, demanded his kisses. He liked how her long auburn hair covered the fullness of her breasts...making Aphrodite seem insignificant.

Reaching out to her, "Where are you off to?"

"The rain...if I don't calm it, it will turn into a torentional storm, flooding the last bit of harvest, and I will only have myself to blame." And with that, she vanished up the stairwell and into the tower of the lighthouse.

When Amias reached the lantern room, Juniper was spinning a spell to the orchestra of thunder. Nothing she said or did surprised him. Unlike Rowan, who was confused and needed to be guided through her awakening, Juniper was in control of her abilities, and her skills were well tuned. Her need for a guardian seemed unnecessary to him, but his need for her may prove to be essential.

Joining her at the window, "Is this your power... controlling the weather?"

Annoyed because he disturbed her, "I am more than just this. Do I control the weather? Not exactly. My emotions appear to control it better than I. Honestly, I thought I had it mastered."

It was beginning to make sense to him. The real reason Rhen seemed familiar to him was because he had seen him in the old paintings at the sanctuary. It had nothing to do with Vardon being his brother, but everything to do with the fact that Juniper's grandfather was and is a descendant of the God of the Northwind, Boreas! And now watching Juniper, her ability to move water, and the way she moves across the floor, solidified his belief.

Turning to Juniper, "I have an idea. I think I know how to calm this emotional storm, but I need your permission to touch you".

"Fine...but how is touching me going to help?"

"Trust me," he whispered.

With their mouths only inches apart he could feel the change in her breathing.

Show me, she thought. Show me what you can do...be the lion. Juniper took a deep breath, then exhaled, lowering her walls that would now allow him to touch her without getting zapped.

Amias placed one hand inside her cardigan, running his fingers over her erect nipples, while his other hand undid the top button, letting his lips linger between her breasts.

Another button, another kiss. Downward he moved.

The storm continued to battle the skies, but it could not compete with the tempest that was raging inside her. She could feel her flower pulsate with an urgency to be released. She's had lovers before, but not like this. None had been able to turn her senses into overdrive, none had given her the orgasm her body demanded. Juniper closed her eyes, running her fingers over his crescent birthmark...and again, it shimmered.

Was it the sweet smell of her musk or the need to compete with the pace of the storm? Whatever it was, Amias couldn't hold back any longer, he needed to feed, and he needed to taste her. In one quick swoop, Amias placed Juniper on the sill, burrowing his face into the warmth between her legs. He wanted to remain surrounded in the softness of her flesh, to tease her, but within moments, and the slip of his tongue, Juniper's storm was set free, releasing the nectar he so desired.

As Juniper continued to sit on the window sill, allowing Amias to lap every drop, the storm ceased and the sky turned to hues of fuschia and gold.

~ Chapter 4 ~

The sun was deceiving. The night storm had removed the remaining leaves, offering the November frost a palette to shimmer on.

Juniper wished she had brought her gloves. The handlebars were cold, making her fingers ache. She tried to stay focused on the list of questions she had for her uncle, and on the peddling of her bike, but last night's events kept clouding her thoughts.

How did he know what to do? She mumbled to herself. Does he know more than what he's telling them? Is it a plan? Juniper had to get some straight answers and soon. The Elder moon was approaching and she wanted to be sure.

Juniper found Rhen deep in old books and thought, while the cat preened himself on the table.

"Looking for something in particular Uncle?"

Rhen leaned back in his chair.

"Perhaps. That was quite a storm last night, it's so unlike you to lose control."

"Stop studying me Uncle, it's unnerving and I didn't lose control."

How dare he question her ability?

Juniper stood in front of the fire, warming her hands. She had to be careful on how to approach him with her list of questions. Whenever she pressed too hard he always went silent, leaving her even more frustrated.

"Do you know who Amais's parents are?"

Rhen joined Juniper by the fire, kissed her on top of her head.

"Is this morning going to be filled with a laundry list of questions?"

"Not if you give me details."

Rhen just smiled and nodded his head in agreement. Taking his place in his favorite chair, "Before we begin, where the guardian is?"

"I left him sleeping in the hammock."

The cat was now pacing around her ankles, rubbing his face against her calves, sometimes stretching his body up her leg, requesting her attention. Juniper rubbed the top of his head, then took a seat before the fire.

"Uncle...why don't you and my father speak?"

Rhen rubbed his long beard, trying to find the words that would satisfy her.

"Let's just say Vardon is an ambitious man with patience."

"That doesn't sound like a bad thing."

The cat now had settled himself in Juniper's lap, purring in his contentment.

"No. Not always...but, those he paid homage to, had or have, ill intentions. Remember, not all Gods are good."

"And Amias's father?"

Rhen's stomach began to grumble.

"Do you plan on feeding me during this inquisition?"

Juniper laughed, "Of course, but not until you answer more questions. Then I'll make some porridge with honey. And... if you answer in detail, I may add fruit."

Surrendering to her, "Amias's father is King Erik. He could have been a great man, but unfortunately he took heed from those who were blinded by greed and power."

In response to answering fully, Juniper rose and began cooking.

"Was my father the one whispering ugliness into King Eriks ear?"

"Yes. Vardon was, and is, the wolf in sheep's clothing. I, and a few others attempted to change the course, but fate, nor the Gods would allow us to change what had already been put into motion."

Juniper began slicing apples to add to the porridge.

"And what became of King Erik?"

Eager to eat, Rhen let out a long sigh.

"Is there a reason you are asking all these specific questions?"

"Yes, and if you want food, start yapping."

"Fine. Just this one and then feed me, or I'll refuse to answer any more."

"If you're attempting to be gruff it isn't working, your eyes are too kind."

"According to the members of council that still come here, King Erik died under mysterious circumstances."

Juniper knew there was more. Her curiosity and need for explanations was making her anxious.

As she was reminding herself that with anxiety comes a change in the weather, the front door blew open. A gust of November cold blew brittle leaves into the room followed by Amias.

"Perfect timing my boy!"

Rhen stood to greet Amias, then turned to Juniper with a smile.

"If you think we are done you are mistaken," she scolded.

Juniper sat the tray of porridge and coffee on the table.

Turning to Amias, "Maybe you can give me some detail to my uncle's answers. He is useless when he has an empty belly."

"I can't help it. It's hard to think when the bear is growling," he chirped.

"Amias, you best eat too. My niece is going to be in our ear until she thinks she has uncovered something."

Amias poured himself a cup of coffee.

"Thank you, but while I was out exploring, I was asked to break bread with your woodsman, Ivar, and his family."

Between bites, "Ah yes, Ivar...good man, lots of talent. You should see the boats he builds. His craftsmanship makes the Gods proud."

Juniper watched her uncle's bowl. For the first time she wished he would eat faster. There was no time for idle chatter about boats and what types of wood works best. There were too many voids, and she needed answers. Juniper grabbed Rhen's spoon midair, scooped up the bowls and brought them directly to the kitchen.

"Don't mind her. You came in the midst of her inquiry and she gets bossy when interrupted."

"I find it quite charming, her bossiness."

"Charming? That's one way of putting it."

Juniper re-entering the room. "Maybe you could shed some light on my questions then?"

I'd rather be kissing you, he thought to himself.

"I'll do my best, my Lady."

Rhen winced.

"First, do not address me that way. Second, how did your father, King Erik, die?"

"I don't know. My father died and his death was blamed on me. Now, I may not have agreed on how he started running the realm, but I did not kill him."

Juniper watched as her uncle stroked his beard. Something he always does when pondering. His wheels were turning.

Taking advantage of the stillness, Juniper took Amias's hands and led him to a stool that she had placed it in front of the fire. She liked the way he looked at her and the hint of violet in his eyes. Caressing his face, she hoped he would forgive her for what she was about to do, for the line of questioning yet to come.

Amias wrapped his arms around her thighs, enjoying the warmth of her hands on his face. He needed her to believe him. He needed her to understand why he behaved so badly. How he no longer held those beliefs, that it was she he believed in now.

Juniper kissed him lightly, and took a deep breath.

"Uncle snap out of it, I need to show you something." gesturing to Amias's neck.

"Why do I feel like some specimen that's about to be dissected?"
Amias questioned

Juniper pointed to the crescent birthmark.

"Uncle, now watch what happens when I touch it."

Juniper gently brushed her fingers over the crescent, making it shimmer while sending a pleasurable sensation throughout her and Amias's bodies.

Rhen did not react the way Juniper thought he should have. Instead, he was calm and not at all taken by surprise at the sight.

"Amias, do you have any idea what is on the back of your neck?"

"If I did, do you think I would be this uncomfortable?"

"And no one ever told you about this birthmark?"

"No. Why is it such a big deal?"

Rhen's eyes scanned Juniper. He knew what she was thinking.

"The depth of your birthmark and what it may mean, may be a bigger deal, depending on which road you choose."

Rhen nodded knowingly at Juniper, then patted Amias on the shoulder, "I think we could use a drink."

Settled in a chair with a snifter of cognac, Amias's tension began to lessen. He wasn't sure he wanted to hear what Rhen had to say. Sometimes not knowing is best. He watched as Juniper settled herself near the fire. He loved the way the light danced in her hair, and the way her sweater hung off her shoulder, daring him to kiss it. The cat had been watching him, watching her. He would have sworn the cat could read his mind, because no sooner had he imagined kissing Juniper, the cat, discovering her open lap, climbed in, but not before rubbing his face against hers and licking her shoulder.

"Before I begin," Rhen started, "you must know that what I'm about to tell you I cannot be sure of."

Rhen began to pack his pipe.

"Amias, I believe you when you say you had nothing to do with your father's death. I also believe that my brother, Vardon, needed you to take the fall to keep eyes off him."

"But why Uncle? What could my father possibly gain from King Erik's death?"

"When I was still part of the realm things had begun to change in the outside world. The water was becoming polluted, the air quality was contaminated and modern technology had begun poisoning everything, including the fertility of its, and our population. That's when Vardon made a deal with the Gods."

Rhen paused, releasing a ring of smoke. He watched as Amias and Juniper sat wide-eyed, like children around a campfire telling ghost stories. Holding their breath, waiting to jump at the slightest sound. He was tempted to say he was done, just to hear them beg for more.

"He should have known not to make a deal with the Gods. Gods are fickle and have a habit of changing outcomes. Vardon asked the Gods to make him King, and in return, he would give them a daughter, a goddess to heal their earth."

"I don't understand. My father has two sons, why would Vardon think he'd be king? Amias asked.

"You, Amias, were first in line for the throne, and for reasons I'm not 100% sure of, unable to control. So...Vardon focused on your brother, Keelen. If he could get Keelen on the throne, then he could reign through him."

"It's impossible to control Keelen. He may seem aloof but he doesn't take orders."

"Oh he didn't plan on controlling him. He planned on using his daughter to do the dirty work. What man, under the spell of a goddess, would not do whatever is asked to keep their love?"

Juniper's heart was racing as her uncle unfolded the truth of her existence. Never before had he mentioned such things, and never before had she questioned her own purpose. For that reason alone, Juniper decided that wine would make it easier and it would keep her emotions on a steady plateau. Deciding against a goblet, Juniper drank from the bottle while pacifying the cat with belly rubs.

Amias, pondering his question, nodded his head and watched as Juniper drank from the bottle of wine. He wished they were alone. Watching her full mouth surround the bottle and drink brought back images of their evening in the tub, and how she skillfully and eagerly drank from him.

The cat meowed as Juniper disrupted his nap by moving. He envied the cat.

Another smoke ring, another swig of wine. Rhen continued.

"The Gods, on the other hand, have another plan. I don't think Vardon knows that Isleen gave birth to twins. Honestly...I don't think even Isleen knows she has two living daughters."

Turning his attention to Amias.

"Do you know who your mother is?"

"Sadly, no. I was told that my parents were united briefly and that she died during childbirth."

Rhen went back to stroking his beard, getting lost in his thoughts.

~ Chapter 5 ~

The setting sun cast shades of orange across the cloudless sky, making their walk through the village appear as though it was painted with the oils of an artist.

Juniper was glad she left her bike at her uncle's. With the amount of wine she had consumed, there was no way she would have been able to gracefully navigate herself on two wheels. She could tell that the temperature had dropped by the visual the air made when she breathed. Her body, on the other hand, was warm and her head fuzzy. She needed food.

Amias remained silent as he walked beside her, only reaching for her from time to time, when she began to stagger. He found it amusing that her airy way of walking had turned into stumbles, taking note not to allow her to drink too much wine from now on. He wanted to ask her if everything she learned today had changed the way she saw him. The way she felt, if she felt anything at all.

At an attempt to keep the cold air from stinging her face, Juniper began walking backwards.

With her eyes fixed on Amias, "Now that you know the truth, will you be leaving?"

Amias was about to answer when the caw of a raven caught their attention, causing her to trip backwards, only to be saved with his quick response.

Holding on to the nape of her cloak, Amias pulled Juniper into his arms. The sweet smell of wine filled his nostrils as he breathed in her essence. As unsure as he was about her question, and how to answer it, he was far from being unsure about how he was feeling at that moment. He wanted her.

The raven cawed again, drawing Amias's attention to the large tree is sat in.

"The witch has returned" she whispered

Amais wasn't about to let a witch, Odin, or any other God disrupt his plight. To be sure Juniper was giving him permission, he pulled her even closer, opening her mouth with his tongue, while simultaneously reaching under her skirt. She was warm and wet, and his fingers played easily on her clit.

Not wanting to, but needing to, Amias pulled away. He could wait and take her home, he thought. But he needed to seize the moment now. Throwing Juniper over his shoulder he headed to the tree where the raven sat.

Juniper submitted willingly. She was so used to being the one that dominated, she found his take charge attitude refreshing and arousing.

He couldn't get his hands on her quick enough. Up against the trunk of the tree, and her legs wrapped around his waist, Juniper helped Amias expose her breasts to the evening air and the warmth of his mouth. As he sucked and nipped at her nipples, both of his hands were under her dress, massaging her ass with one hand as the fingers of the other slid in and out.

This new sensation caused Juniper to moan with delight and ache with the need to have him inside her. For a split second she worried if he would be able to handle what was about to happen, and then his mouth was back on hers.

No words needed to be spoken. Amias anticipated her response, and within seconds he was guiding his hard cock, pushing slowly until his entire shaft had disappeared.

"Harder Amias, harder," she whispered between kisses.

Doing what she asked of him, Amias continued to plunge his cock deeper and deeper, as his body was overcome with an electrical current emitted by her.

Juniper watched Amias's face as the current ran through them. Any normal man would have fainted or blacked-out from the shock, but not her lion. It only made him fuck her faster, giving her the satisfying pounding she begged him for.

Her mentor had tried to explain what would happen when she finally connected with another like her, but words couldn't explain how the magnetic charge would feel. It was a pleasurable pain, stronger than a tingle, leaving her thirsting for more.

In sync with the caw of the raven, Amias held onto her pumping hips and rode Juniper's wave of elation until every ounce was spilled, and the snow began to fall.

~ Chapter 6 ~

"Did we cause this?" Amais asked as he re-entered the room with an arm full of wood.

"The snow? Perhaps...or it's falling because it's the end of November." Juniper had moved a slab of tree stump near the fireplace, placing upon it, two bowls of onion soup, and a plate with cheese, bread and pomegranate.

She liked his company and how he tended to her needs. Normally she would have been the one chopping wood and starting the fire. And earlier, when he insisted on bathing her when they returned, kissing her body as he did, flickered something inside her that was beyond lust.

Taking his place near her, Amias began to eat. He had always enjoyed food, but tonight the flavor was stronger.

"How do you feel about what my uncle told you?"

"It was a relief to know that there are others who aren't blaming me for my father's death."

"Yes, that must be a relief. I, on the other hand, found it very disturbing that my own father attempted to deceive the Gods. As if they wouldn't know he had no intention to use his daughter for the good of the human race, to heal Mother Earth, but as a tool for his own greed."

Amias fed her a pomegranate seed, "I'm so sorry. You should never feel as though you are just a tool in some wicked game. You are so much more than that, and deserve to be treated with respect."

No sooner did Juniper kiss his fingers, licking the fruit juices off his fingertips, the tingling sensation started. She wanted to go with the feeling but pushed it aside.

"What do you plan on doing now that you know Keelen isn't the one that should be sitting on the throne?"

"Good question. I think I should warn him and Rowan what Vardon is up to, but as far as the throne...I have always wanted to take my father's place, to rule, to be a King above all Kings."

Something sank inside Juniper. She had experienced loss before. The loss of a pet, a friend, but never the loss of a man. She had never let her walls down to have a partner, and now, with Amias and the fear of what he was about to tell her, made her feel as though there was a hole inside her. She did not like this form of sadness.

Reaching over, and pulling Juniper into his lap, Amias continued.

"I need to confess something to you. I have done things I am not proud of and I'm afraid once you learn of them, you will see me in a different light."

"Remember when I was cutting your hair and I said it symbolized the separation from your past? I meant that. There isn't anything you could possibly say that would shock me or make me turn a cheek. Answer me this. If you knew what you know now, would you have done the things you did?"

"No, but had I not, then I wouldn't have gone through the veil and arrived here."

"Well...not necessarily. I think there is more to your story."

Juniper stood up, and began clearing the dishes, but before she could get halfway across the room, she stopped and turned to Amias, who was now leaning back on his elbows, staring into the fire. "Do you feel as though you have lost your purpose? I mean...we have been training our entire lives for something big. You, as a guardian of earth's fountain, to educate on her abilities, and I? I have no fucking clue anymore."

Amias sat up. He could tell she was doing her damndest to hold it together, and found it best to just remain silent.

Fighting back her tears of frustration, Juniper continued to the kitchen. Only to return with an opened bottle of wine, "From the time I could walk my mentor and my uncle have been getting me ready for your arrival. I have been educated, my skills finely tuned and my gifts enhanced, and to find out I don't have to be Queen, is...quite frankly, a fucking relief."

"Really? That surprises me considering how well you command a room."

Through more sips of wine and a giggle, "Your sarcasm is appreciated."

"May I?" Amias extended his hand for the bottle.

"Yes, of course. Best you keep that away from me, too much muddles my self-control." Taking the bottle,"Have you really read all those books?"

Still standing above him. "Nice change of subject."

"I really want to be under your nightgown, but I figured with your wine consumption over the past several hours, it was best to re-direct."

Motioning him to "hold that thought", Juniper dragged a down filled pillow over to where Amias was sitting and plopped herself down. "Did you know that you can see the changes in the world through the books one reads? What society found precious in the 13th century is completely different from what has been written in the 80's."

There was a passionate dance between her hand gestures and facial expressions as she spoke, and Amias found himself becoming mesmerized.

"Hey!" Juniper snapped her fingers. "Are you hearing anything I'm saying?"

He hadn't. "Yes, of course."

"Do you know the one thing that becomes the downfall?"

"I don't know, what?"

Juniper repositioned herself, "Man, man himself. He, or she, becomes his own enemy. The greed for power and control and individualism, it's the downfall of the human race.

You see, as they attempt to reach what they think they desire, they destroy themselves and the earth in the process."

Now climbing into Amias's lap so her lips hovered near his, "Our Gods are being replaced with material wealth, poisons, and a dozen other things. We are forgotten, and soon we will no longer exist."

Her words frightened him because he knew they were true.

"Then I guess we have some work to do...in the meantime..." Amias moved his hand to the base of her back, drawing her closer. The smell of wine on her breath was intoxicating, stirring a desire to drink off of her. After several kisses and love bites, Amias removed Juniper's gown, "Hand me the wine."

Juniper leaned over and handed him the bottle.

"Will you do me the honor of laying down?"

He had piqued her curiosity. She liked the tone of his voice and how he put his commands in the form of a question. Had any other man asked her in such a manner she would have refused. The warrior inside of her would have sent an uncomfortable shock at the first touch, and she would remain in control.

Amias rose and began searching the cupboards and when he found what he was looking for, returned.

Warming the contents of the jar in his hands, Amias started massaging her feet. The scent of sandalwood grew stronger as he kneaded the muscles below.

Juniper placed her foot on his chest so he could work on her calf, "That feels really good. I could get used to this."

Amias just smiled. "Earlier you whispered the witch had returned. What did you mean by that?"

"My mentor, Anise. She has returned from her travels."

"I know so little of your awakening, I'm jealous. Tell me about her."

"Only if you're magic hands continue."

He now began working on her thighs. "Of course."

"Anise brought me here when I was born and cared for me as though I was her own. You'd like her. She's soft spoken, gentle and very wise."

Amias had now reached the top of her thighs. Massaging each one with care, purposely running the tips of his fingers between them, dipping one every now and again inside to feel her wetness.

"Is that it? She must be of great skill to have been entrusted in your education."

"Is there a method to your madness?" Juniper lifted her hips in hopes he would go deeper. He didn't.

"Madness? Are you implying my massage is driving you mad?"

"You know exactly what you are doing to me."

Licking his fingertips, "yes...yes I do. And if you want more, tell me more."

"Fine, I surrender."

"Good." Amias's hands resumed his exploration. With one hand he began rubbing the curvature of her hips as the other, began massaging her clit in circular motions.

Through clenched teeth Juniper struggled to answer. "Do you know of Artemis?"

"Yes, the goddess of the hunt." Amias licked each erect nipple, his hands unfaltering.

"This is torture!"

Amias stopped what he was doing and gave her a wicked but seductive smile.

"Alright, alright...don't stop. Artemis is the goddess of the hunt, but also of fertility, and child-birth. Anise is her descendant and..." Amias was now darting his tongue inside her well as his hands fondled her breasts. Her breathing now heavy, "I need to feel your hardness inside me.., oh god...this feels so good."

Again, Amias stopped. Juniper thought for sure he was going to deny her what she sought.

"Do you want more Juniper?"

"Isn't it obvious?"

Amias lifted her hips so they were resting on his thighs. He liked having her squirm for more, it made him feel strong and desired. Bending her knees, he opened her up, taking in the world he longed to stay. Slowly he teased the outside of her slit, rubbing his engorged head in her wetness, only slipping in the tip, then pulling back out.

"How do you want it Juniper?" Deeper with the tip, then back out.

"Do with me what you will, just don't stop," she begged.

One deep thrust and Juniper was rocking her hips, then back out.

"Do you want more?"

"Yes"

"I want you to keep telling more as we climax." Thrusting with each syllable, "You like books, which means you like words. Words, can be so erotic."

Juniper did what was asked of her. She knew it would only be moments before she would be Cumming and tightening around the girth of his manhood.

"The Goddess is symbolized..."

Amias's eyes never left her. He watched as the red flush covered her chest and creeped into her face. Thrusting deeper, spreading her wider so she could welcome his seed, Amias began to pulsate with an electrical current,

Increasing his rhythm.

"Her symbol is the crescent moon." Juniper let out a satisfying scream that rippled across the sea, followed by echoes of jubilation.

Did he hear her right? Amias waited until Juniper's breathing had steadied before questioning her. "Did you just say crescent?"
"Ssshhhhh, you've exhausted me. No time for talk, only time for sleep" and with that, Juniper got up and crawled into her bed, leaving Amias with unanswered questions and naked in front of the fire.

~ Chapter 7 ~

No matter how well he bundled up, Amias couldn't escape the Northern cold. Shoving his hands inside his coat pockets, Amias shivered as he headed back to the lighthouse. It had been two weeks since he woke to find Juniper gone. She had left a note saying she needed to see Anise and that she would explain everything on her return, but the fact that she just left without telling him in person made him feel anxious. Something was coming, he could feel it in his bones, and not even the solitude of the island could keep it at bay.

"Amias! Hey, I'm glad I caught you."

Amias looked up to see Ivar jogging towards him. His face red from the cold air.

Stopping, then adjusting his scarf, "What can I help you with?"

"It's more like, what can I do for you."

"Oh? Do tell."

"My wife thinks you have been spending too much time alone and could probably use a hot meal and company." Ivar paused briefly, pulling his wool cap farther down. "And I have to agree with her. Care to join us for dinner?"

"I would like that. I'm not much of a cook and the thought of eating something other than salted fish and crackers sounds wonderful."

Ivar's face beamed, "You have no idea how happy that makes me. Had I returned and you weren't with me, I would never have heard the end of it."

Amias put his arm around Ivar's shoulder, "You're safe from your wife's wrath." Both men laughed, and for a few hours Amias wouldn't have to live inside his head.

Ivar and his wife had fed him well on food and conversation. As the two men laughed over a pint and stories of the Gods, something caught Amias's eye.

Pointing toward the shelf on the wall, "May I take a better look?"

Ivar looked to where Amias was pointing, then retrieved it.

Handing the box to him, "I made this for my Lily in celebration of Lupercalia. We were newly bound and any help from the fertility Gods was welcomed." Then with a sweep of his arm, "Three lads and a lass...the gods have been good."

Amias ran his hand over the delicacy of the wooden box. He could tell that Ivar had put more than hard work into it. In the center he had carved a Celtic knot and inlaid the rest with small seashells and pearls.

Handing it back to Ivar, "It's beautiful."

"Thanks." Beaming with pride, Ivar placed it back on the shelf.

"I'd like to make one...for Juniper. Could you lend me some tools and instruct me?"

"Really?" Ivar and Lily looked at each other, then back at Amias.

"Why do you both seem puzzled?"

Lily spoke first. Clearing her throat and reaching for words, "We're just surprised that you would want to offer such a heartfelt gift considering..."

Ivar jumped in to rescue his wife, "Considering she is untouchable."

Internally, Amias was gloating, "Why would you say such a thing?"
Lily walked over to where the two men were sitting and filled their
cups, "I'm going to leave the rest of the conversation between the two
of you." Lily thanked Amais for breaking bread with them, stating he
was welcome anytime, then kissed Ivar, bidding them a good night.
Ivar's eyes searched the room, then assured that no one was in ear
shot, he continued, "It has been said that Juniper turns men to ash.
That everytime she takes a lover, she kills him as soon as
consummation begins. She's like the black widow." Ivar took a pause,
trying to read Amias's face, "I'm really sorry to have to tell you that,
but I would be really careful. For your and your peckers sake."
Amias's laughter turned into a roar, tears running down his face, "I,
and my prick, can assure you that we are living proof of survival."
Laughing and shaking his head, Amias rose to take his leave. "Thank
you for tonight friend, I'll come by your shop tomorrow."

A fresh blanket of snow had fallen, and as the wind whipped it
through the air, the moonlight lit each flake like lightning bugs in
summer. Amias wasn't keen on the cold weather, and missed the
conveniences of the modern world. A car with heat would be really
handy right about now and running hot water.
He wasn't sure if it was the wind, with the mix of snow playing tricks,
but moving, like watercolor running in the rain, Amias noticed a
figure near the lighthouse, causing his heart to flip, sending an elated
feeling of joy through his body. Could it be Juniper? Quicker he
moved toward the image, only to watch as the same gust that pressed

against him, attempting to slow his pace, fractured the vision into tiny colors of light.

****

Juniper paced, wringing her hands. The Elder moon had come and gone and she needed to go home. But not before bringing up the subject of her birth and the events that have taken place while Anise was gone.

Anise had been busy preparing herbs, crushing them with the wooden mortar and pestle, when she noticed Juniper frantically grasping at her thoughts. Anyone looking in would think she was anxious, lost, or perhaps out of control. Anise knew better.

"Are you attempting to wear a moat around my chair?"

Juniper rolled her eyes, joining Anise at the table, "I need to tell you something and I'm trying to figure out in which order."

"I suggest picking one moment and starting from it's beginning."

Juniper's body relaxed, she knew her so well.

"While you were gone a guardian arrived through a veil that he didn't choose."

Anise stopped what she was doing.

Juniper searched Anise's face, her soft dark eyes, for some kind of reaction. She hadn't noticed when she first arrived, but now, as the rays of sunlight pushed through the window, she could see faint lines of wisdom on her face and the silver streaks in her long black hair now framed her.

"Rhen thought he was mine, but after we listened to the guardian's story, he already had a charge."

Anise rose and began making two cups of tea. She now had questions of her own but refrained, in case there was more to be revealed. Juniper added honey, stirring the spoon with a wave of her finger. Taking a sip, Anise gestured to Juniper to continue.

"His charge lured him into the "in between". He believes she slipped him an herb for sleep. Then left him there, closing the veil behind her."

"So this charge, is she roaming with no direction?"

"I don't think so. I do, however, feel as though she is going to be manipulated to do the bidding of my father, Vardon. And, to add another twist to this story, the guardian's charge, looks just like me."

Anise's slowly rose from the table to tend to the fire. No matter how many logs she threw into it, the chill inside her couldn't be reached. Nineteen years she had kept Juniper safe. Safe from a man who's purpose turned from humanity to self-serving, and safe from the poisons of the current world.

It was inevitable she thought as she extended her hand to Juniper. "Come make black cake with me and I will tell you your story."

Juniper began scooping the pomegranate seeds into a large bowl, while Anise gathered the other ingredients. She enjoyed making their version of black cake this time of year, adding dried apricots, apple, and molasses instead of honey, and today was no different.

Juniper knew her path may change, and if she was a normal person, she'd be scared, but no, Juniper found herself positively giddy with excitement.

Anise stopped to take Juniper's hands into hers, "I was your mother's midwife. She did give birth to two daughters. The one born quiet was given the name Rowan, and the one who howled with cries and fists, I named Juniper."

Anise set the dough onto a large round stone, then placed it in the opening, built into the fireplace. Juniper followed.

Anise sat Juniper on the floor in front of where she was sitting. She began brushing her hair, making sure any and all hair that remained in the brush were gathered and placed in a box.

"Your mother, Isleen, knew something was amiss and when I told her what I knew, she handed you to me, knowing I would keep you well and safe from Vardon's wickedness. The word of twins was never sent back to the realm. So your father does not know of your existence."

Juniper looked over her shoulder. "I'm going to assume you had a very good reason for committing such an act."

"I believe I did."

Anise began braiding, weaving ribbon into Juniper's hair.

"Many of us had already begun questioning the direction King Erik was taking our purpose, and could see the change in your father. Vardon would return from the present world with stories of power and industry, of chemicals and new belief systems. And as he embraced these new ideas, the old ways began to fade, and our land started a slow death. That is when I, your uncle and others in the realm decided to leave."

With her hair finished, Juniper turned to face Anise. She loved it when Anise would tell her tales of the old ways, of the Gods and

Goddesses that once walked the earth, and how the intensity in her words would cause her to sit on edge. This story was no different and she didn't want to miss a single syllable.

Anise knew the answer before she asked. She could read it in Juniper's eyes. "You have a question?"

"How did you know I was to be?"

"The day Vardon made his proposal to the Gods I had a vision of sea life and birds floating in oil slicks, dying in a smoke filled sky. And again, on the eve of your conception, a vision of two trees. Both bearing fruit and lush leaves surrounded by death. I knew then that the Gods were giving me the chance to change what your father had begun."

Anise rose from her rocker and proceeded to remove the black cake from the brickoven. The sweet smell filled the room causing Juniper's stomach to growl. Taking that as a cue, Juniper fetched plates, mead, and sliced cheese, quickly returning to her spot on the floor.

Of all the mysteries she had read, this one she thought, was by far the best.

She could see the wonderment in Juniper's eyes as she waited for her to continue. Anise never feared Juniper's reaction, what she did fear was how Juniper was going to come back from the upcoming battle and still retain the belief that the human condition is deserving of the faith she had given it.

Anise took a quick sip of mead. "Where did I leave off?"

With a full mouth of cake and in between chews, Juniper replied, "Your visions and my ass of a father."

"Ah yes…Vardon. He made it easy. He was so absorbed in his deal with the Gods he never checked on your mother. He just planted his seed and left, knowing one day, upon his child's awakening, she would be returned to him to serve his purpose."

The mead was relaxing Juniper's mind and her tongue. "The more you tell me of this man, the more I want to shock the fucker."

Anise chuckled softly. "Well, now that you have put it out there, its fruition is inevitable.

Juniper laid her head down on Anise's lap, allowing her to stroke her face. "I'm not taking this one back."

"I wouldn't expect you to. But, before you go planning, we need to speak with Rhen and the other elders, as how to proceed. A full quiver is needed, if we are to go up against your father."

Juniper wanted to tell her about Amias. The way they connected and his illuminating birthmark, but the day had been filled with enough serious conversation. All she wanted to do now was enjoy being with the woman whom she admired and loved like a mother.

Chapter 8

It was midafternoon when Anise arrived at Rhen's. She had agreed to meet back up with Juniper later on in the evening, but first she needed to address the current situation.

Opening the heavy door, Anise immediately was hit with the warmth of the fire and the sight of Rhen hovering over several leather bound books. The cat, who had been grooming itself, immediately jumped off the table upon seeing her.

Scooping up her feline, "Well aren't you a sight for sore eyes."

"Are you directing that to your cat or to me?" Rhen replied.

"Both I suppose."

"I'm not sure you are going to have the same sediment once I tell you what has happened since you've been gone," he grunted.

"Before you begin to chastise me for not telling you that Juniper is a twin, let me just say that my intention was not to keep you in the dark, but to keep everyone in the dark. Had word gotten to your brother, then there would be no hope at all for mankind."

Looked up from his studies, "I have never questioned your motives, and the new knowledge of a twin doesn't surprise me. What does, however, is that this particular guardian showed up here. It doesn't add up."

Anise took a seat near the fire, allowing the cat to knead itself into a comfortable position on her lap. She too had concerns, but preferred to remain silent, as to not cause unnecessary worry.

Closing the leather bound book, Rhen joined Anise near the fire, offering her a plate of cheese and bread before sitting himself down. Packing his pipe, Rhen broke the silence, "Anise, for centuries you have been my closest companion, and I fully trust you, but something is off. It may be a twist of the Gods, but this guardian has connected with Juniper."

Catching her breath, "Wait...what? Juniper never mentioned anything like that to me."

"Maybe she was so caught up with learning of her birth and finding out she has a twin, she forgot or decided to address that at another time."

"Maybe."

"Does Isleen know you have her other daughter?"

"Yes, yes, of course. I'm not the evil hag living in the woods stealing babies for dinner." Anise winked at Rhen, "Seriously though, Yes, Isleen and her great grandmother, know. We had decided that the only path for the redemption of mankind was to keep one babe away from Vardon. In case he was able to put his self-serving motives into play."

"Do you think the twin, Rowan, would be easily manipulated? I find it unnerving that she tricked her guardian into the in-between, closing the veil, and leaving him behind."

Anise moved the cat onto the floor, causing him to meow from being woken.

"That piece of information has me perplexed as well. Rowan would need her guardian. Unlike Juniper, she didn't have the benefit of being trained and skilled in her specific craft. Her awakening needs guidance, and once she weds, she will need to learn how to control it." Exhaling a circle of smoke, "According to the guardian, Rowan was set to marry right before she trapped him. Do we have a mess that needs to be cleaned up Anise?"

"I hope not. I think the new King will be able to see through any deception from Vardon and contain Rowan's hunger."

Lifting his stein towards Anise, "Here's to hope!"

****

Juniper had been anxious the entire walk home. She had missed him and his constant questions. Seeing how eagerly he absorbed all she taught him gave her a sense of validation. It wasn't that she needed validation from anyone, let alone a man to make her feel as though she had a purpose, but the validation that what she could teach was worthy, gave her a positive indication that she was on the right path. The packed snow under her feet made a crunching noise as she hurried towards the lighthouse. Had he missed her? Or was he vexed at her quick departure? Either way, she would be happy to see him and once they were in the same space, whatever negative thought was in his mind, it would dissipate. That she was sure of.

The lighthouse seemed too still as she approached. Her two Juniper trees, now holding the winter's snow within its branches, reminded her of herself. Holding the future of birth and death in the palms of its hands.

Juniper had imagined walking into her home, Amias there to embrace her and cover her with kisses, but fruitation was not to be. Instead she found it to be empty and cold. Refusing to let her heart get the best of her, Juniper proceeded to warm her home with a fire and tend to the tower.   The winter solstice would be coming soon and she needed to prepare the platform and whale oil. Those coming to the island depended on the light to help guide them through the surrounding waters and aid in the navigation of the rocks and reef. She always enjoyed the many stories the others coming to the island would tell. The objects and inventions they would bring. But most of all, she looked forward to the variety of books they would bring her and the many adventures that lay within its binding. She never grew tired of books and the smell of their pages.

The sun had begun to set and Juniper found it best to keep her mind off the passing hours by baking apples and bread. She figured Amias would return hungry and full of questions. A full stomach would ease his mind.

But as the hours continued to pass Juniper focused her mind on spinning the wool she had picked up on her way home.

Before Amias opened the door to her lighthouse he had planned to be gruff and to chastise her for leaving with just a note. He deserved better, especially after what they had shared the night before! But once he had stepped over the threshold, Amias's negative feelings soon dissipated as the sweet smell of cinnamon apples and bread filled his nostrils and the sight of Juniper's grace as she spun and peddled the wool.

Amias closed the heavy door, removed his coat and scarf and walked towards Juniper "Just when I think I've grown used to your beauty, you enchant me all over again."

Juniper stopped spinning and slowly turned to face him. An overwhelming relief crossed her face with a broad smile, "You're not too shabby yourself."

Amias was now standing over her, placing her face into his hands, "Before I indulge in the deliciousness of your cooking I must first taste the sweetness of those lips."

Her mouth was warm and inviting, and as much as he wanted to continue to kiss her gently, his hunger quickened with the darting of her tongue.

Juniper reached up, wrapping her arms around his neck, pulling him closer. She could feel the tingling, like an electrical current begin to flood her body and she wanted more.

Sensing her willingness, Amias scooped Juniper up off the stool and carried her over to the bookshelf ladder, where he placed her on a rung.

Juniper's hands were in his hair and her lips still connected to his when he ripped open her cardigan, sending buttons flying. His hand movements were rough as they squeezed her breast, bringing each nipple into his mouth, biting lightly and sucking fully.

Soft moans escaped Juniper's lips as he tore away her skirt and soaked panties, leaving her naked, but for a pair of knee highs, on the ladder.

Amias wanted to take in her full beauty and the flush of her skin but his body, like a magnet, couldn't pull away. He needed to taste her, to feel the softness of her flesh tighten on his tongue as he plunged it deep inside her. As if she could read his thoughts, Juniper grabbed onto the rails of the ladder, offering herself up for pleasure.

The time away had left her body aching for his touch and her mind dizzy with responsibilities. She needed to decompress and he was the perfect stress reliever.

Juniper's grip on the rails became tighter as she grinded her pelvis against his darting tongue and open mouth. Her back arched when his hands feverishly teased within her wetness, creating an ache that could only be satisfied with the hardness of his cock.

Amias, aware of her urgency pulled his head away, and with one quick motion, placed one of Juniper's legs over his shoulder, the other around his waist, and began pumping. At first, it was long, even movements as Juniper's body adjusted to his girth. But what sent him into overdrive was the tone of her ordering, "Stop being so tender," in his ear. Harder and harder he pounded. Books began to topple from the shelves in unisense. With short, quick thrusts Juniper's orgasm was finally his, just as his, was hers.

The pulsating rhythm of the eclectic current that ran through them, caused the sky to flash sending a cascade of sleet down upon the island.

Juniper laid her head on Amias's shoulder, lightly kissing it as he carried her to the bed. She had never shared her bed, or her home with a man. Just the thought used to frighten her, but not now. Now she found something harmonious in the idea and welcomed the warmth of his body within her sheets.

With heavy eyes, Juniper fell asleep to Amias stroking her hair and whispering, "If you leave me again, I'm going with you."

~ Chapter 9 ~

Juniper sat straight up covered in sweat, her heart pounding so loud she could hear the blood pulsing through her veins. She tried to remember what exactly it was in her dream that had now caused her fright, but the only pictures she could recollect were the cawing of the raven and the loss of her teeth.

Immediately, and without thought of Amias, Juniper bolted from the warmth of her bed and out into the winter morn. She hardly noticed she was barefoot and knee deep in snow, as she scanned her beloved trees.

No, this can't be. Not now.

Amias had been adding kindle to warm the room, when a gust of wind came out of nowhere, putting out the flame. Immediately turning in the direction of the movement he caught the flash of Juniper and then an open door.

Grabbing his coat and hurrying behind her.

"What's going on Juniper?" Amias was concerned, he could see how feverishly she searched the tree branches.

"It was an omen," she whispered. Then, on hands and knees, she began sifting her hands through the snow.

"What are you looking for?"

"My teeth. My teeth fell out of my mouth in my dream." Her hands were now numb.

"I don't understand? You're looking for your teeth?"

"It's an omen. When one's teeth fall out it means death." Turning her face upward, "I really don't have time for your questions. I would think you would have some kind of knowledge...didn't they teach you the old ways of our people?"

Juniper took a deep breath. She knew her harshness towards him was unwarranted.

Leaning back on her heels, "I'm sorry. I didn't mean to speak down to you."

"It's all good." Extending his hand, "As for your extremities, I'm not so sure of. Your lips are blue."

She knew he was right. Taking another look at her trees, everything seemed to be in its place, perhaps she misread the omen.

Amias sat on the floor leaning his back against the vat of warm water as Juniper soaked her limbs back to life inside it.

She could tell he had questions by the way he kept rubbing his hands over his scalp. Men are so silly she thought. Why they feel the need to dance around any subject is just plain annoying. Taking another sip of the warm cider he had given her, Juniper decided to break the silence.

"If you continue to rub your head like that you'll be bald before noon."

Giving her a side smirk, "What? You don't find bald men attractive?"

"Not if their heads are full of fluff."

Leaning forward and resting her chin on the edge of the tub, Juniper's eyes locked with his. She could tell by his clenched jaw that his concern was getting the best of him.

Speaking in a soft voice, "Spit it out."

"I'm worried Juniper. If your behavior or dream was coming from some other person, I would chalk it up to naivety, but you're the first demi-goddesses, slash wiccan I have ever met, and I highly doubt your omens or gut feelings are ever off."

Amias searched her face, hoping she would tell him that she was mistaken, that everything was going to be alright, but he knew better. Something was coming.

Juniper leaned over and placed a light kiss on his mouth, but before she could pull back Amias had his hands on the back of her head pulling her closer as his full lips crashed against hers. What was supposed to be a kiss to soothe his nerves, had only charged aflame burning in both of them.

Amias couldn't kiss her hard enough. His tongue couldn't search for hers more eagerly.
Pulling her head back by her hair. "I'm going to make you orgasm so hard, there won't be any bad dreams left inside of you."
He didn't give her time to verbally respond. His mouth was back on hers, as his right hand slid between her thighs. Juniper moaned into his mouth when his fingers dipped inside her folds. He wanted to hear her scream his name, to beg him to fill her with his now engorged cock. He'd be damned if he was going to let whatever trick the Gods were playing to ruin what he had only dreamt about in his youth. Amias lifted Juniper out of the tub.

He continued to play inside her until he placed her on the bed. Rolling her over onto her stomach, then lifting her ass up so he could get at her better, Amias began sucking on her clit, his fingers spreading her folds open so his tongue could swirl in and out.

He planned on taking it slow, to imprint this moment so he could return to it later and smile, but Juniper's body had other plans. A low moan, then a melody of passion escaped her, causing the front door to fly open with such force it came off its hinges.

Amis and Juniper both jumped away from the sound.

"What the hell?" Amias pulled on his pants. Smiling, "Damn babe, your enthusiasm for my performance is going to give me a big head and a lot of work."

Throwing a blanket around herself. "That wasn't me."

"Of course it was you. You always affect the weather with your emotions."

Amias walked over to the door and began fiddling with it, trying to get it back in place before snow drifts entered the house.

How dare him! She thought. I am not an emotional weather manipulator!

Juniper grabbed a pair of white wool pants and a navy turtleneck. If he wants emotion, I'll give him emotion! In a huff she began getting dressed.

Amias noticed her changed demeanor. It was obvious he had struck a chord. The way she was aggressively putting on her socks and blowing her hair out of her face made him chuckle.

Standing with her hands on her hips, "What is so funny?"

"Nothing. You just look cute all aggravated." Giving her a quick wink.

Juniper exhaled, relaxing her shoulders. "I'm just antsy."

Amis stopped fiddling with the door. "It was just a bad dream. Can you help me get this closed?"

Juniper screamed.

Now wide eyed and pointing. "I told you it was an omen!!"

A large raven stepped over the threshold dropping a twig at Juniper's feet. Cawing several times.

Juniper knelt down, picking up the twig without breaking eye contact with the bird.

The visit of the raven was giving her mixed signals. If it wasn't for her dream, she would accept its appearance as a prophecy with no ill intent, but now she was absolutely certain it was associated with a lost soul, or even worse, death.

Rolling the twig between her fingers, the raven cawed several more times before taking flight out into the morning sky. A shiver ran down her spine.

Still eyeing the twig. "We need to go...NOW!"

Juniper didn't wait for Amias to break from his frozen posture. Instead, she hurried with lacing up her boots and grabbing her cloak, with the twig still in hand.

"Are you coming or not?" snapping her fingers in front of his face.

"Yes, yes, of course!"

Amias pulled on his boots, gathered his coat and scarf, put the door back in its place, then scurried to catch up with Juniper, who was now power walking towards town.

Catching up with her, "Where are we heading?"

"I have to go see Anise. And if I know her as well as I think I do, she will be at my uncle's place."

"That was really crazy back there, huh?"

"I don't think crazy is the correct word, I would say alarming, but not crazy."

"Can I see the twig?"

Juniper handed him the twig without slowing her pace.

"Oh fuck." Amias immediately knew what he was holding, and the reason for her distress. "This is not good."

"Oh you think?" Juniper never looked his way. She was on a mission and didn't need all his sexyness distracting her.

Handing her back the twig, he shoved his hands into his coat pockets only to pull out pieces of the talisman she had given him the first day they met. Amias couldn't catch his breath, it was now caught in his throat.

"They are thought to be a powerful talisman,
It is said that if one breaks that the power inside them
Was used up protecting a life."

Amias quickly put his hand back in his pocket. He didn't need to add more to this now tumultuous situation.

A hurricane began blowing through his mind, destroying all that it came in contact with, including his future with Juniper.

******

Juniper was determined to take charge of this situation. She was done sitting idly by for answers and there was no way in hell she was going to let the Gods dictate how she would live her life and whom she would live it with. She was now livid.

Amias wasn't surprised to see Rhen's door fly open as they neared it. Juniper's fears had turned to anger and she was now directing that energy towards objects. He liked that she was a bad-ass with her powers, but definitely, wouldn't want to be her target.

Storming into the house and directing herself at Rhen, "I would think twice before you pipe in with a sarcastic tone about me not having my emotions in check."

Rhen open his mouth to speak, then thought better of it when he locked eyes with Amias, warning him to tread lightly with her.

Scanning the large room, "Where is Anise?"

Anise appeared in the doorway of the kitchen, wiping her hands on the apron wrapped around the waist of her red gown. The cat followed at her heels, stopping in front of her, guarding her from Juniper's energy.

She had been grinding up ginger when the North wind blew in Juniper and blew out the candle light.

Juniper rushed over, holding up the twig.

"What am I supposed to do with this?"

Anise raised one eyebrow. "How did you acquire this?"

"A raven. A big black raven came cawing into my house after the Gods blew my door off its hinges. It laid it at my feet and then flew away."

The expression on Anise's face never changed. She knew the raven would be coming, she just didn't know when.

"What makes you think this is significant?"

Juniper rolled her eyes. She hated when Anise would play therapist, why couldn't she just give her the damn answers instead of making her find them inside of herself.

"Why do YOU think it's significant?"

Anise plucked the twig from Juniper's fingers. "It appears from your attitude that there is more than just a raven and twig that has got your panties in a bunch."

"A lot more and it has me unraveling."

"Because you aren't in control?"

"Yet. I'm not in control YET."

Anise moved passed her, carrying the twig over to Rhen. In the midst of Juniper's lack of confidence, she hadn't noticed Amias standing in the shadows, watching like a hoot owl.

Turning to his figure, "You must be the guardian that I've heard about. Please... step out into the light so I may see what has caught my Juniper's eye."

Pictures of his infancy flickered, reminding him of the old silent movies he had seen. Amias knew her, and the longer he watched her the more his birthmark tingled. Standing in the shadows he felt like a child hiding behind the skirt of their mother, scared of the unfamiliar, yet...was she? Amias stepped out into the room.

~ Chapter 10 ~

Juniper and Rhen had been watching the slow motion exchange between Amias and Anise with curiosity. The cat, however, had found a spider to play with, no longer needing to stand guard.

Anise reached for Amias, her hands on both sides of his face, searching his eyes for a glimmer of recognition.

"You've grown."

Amias's voice was just above a whisper, "I have this strong feeling that I know you."

Anise reached behind his neck, pressing the tips of her fingers on Amias's crescent birthmark.

The old silent film began racing. Every memory, every emotion Anise held was now vibrating through his body, reaching and settling in his very core, filling him, making him whole. Tears, no longer dormant, began to flow.

Anise removed her hands when his legs could no longer hold. She was certain he now held all the answers to his questions. All her memories, her pain, her joy, her gifts, their Goddess.

Amias fell to his knees. "Mother?"

"Yes, my sweet boy. I am your mother and now you know why I had to leave you behind. Forgive me?"

A loud roar of laughter escaped Rhen, shattering the moment.

He was never good at tact, Juniper thought to herself, but holy hell, this was some outrageous information and she wasn't sure if she should be in shock, or just join in with her own laughter. Could this day get any stranger?

Rhen continued to laugh so hard he could hardly catch his breath. Wiping tears from his face, he motioned Juniper to grab him a drink.

"I don't see what so funny Uncle is." Handing him a tall stout and his pipe.

Still trying to gather his composure.

"Oh Anise...you sure know how to stir things up with the Gods!" More laughter.

"How long did you know, old man?" Anise shot back. She was not amused by his rendition of a laughing hyena. This was a serious matter.

Throwing up his hands in surrender, "I didn't put two and two together until Juniper showed me his crescent birthmark. And...I stress this, I didn't know he was your son, I only knew he was linked to you somehow."

It was Juniper's turn to interject. Her questions, now a mile high.

"So this entire time you knew? Oh my goddess, this is insane. Why did you keep this from me Uncle? When I showed you his birthmark that day and how it reacted to my touch you said nothing."

Turning to Anise, "And you... how could you keep this from me?"

Anise looked to Rhen for support.

Noting her signals, Rhen walked over to Amias, who was still in a puddle of shock, helped him off the floor, and guided him to one of the chairs in front of the fire.

"It appears we are about to have a hefty conversation, and Juniper, since you know I'm at my best with a full stomach, would you mind whipping something up?"

"Uncle, really? Food? With everything we have just learned your only thought is food?"

"And drink. Don't forget. Drink," Rhen added.

"I'll help you Juniper," Anise offered. "I'm sure you and I could use some alone time." Anise could see her hesitation. "Amias will be just fine, trust me."

Trust you? Juniper was irritated, and trust was not a word in her vocabulary at the moment. However, she did have a lot of questions and the mention of food made her stomach growl.

"Fine! I'll feed your gut Uncle but I expect details...not those one liners you're famous for."

Patting his stomach, Rhen's smile broadened, turning the tension in the room to one of ease.

Leaving the two men in the main room, Juniper and Anise began preparing a platter filled with fruits, some nuts, cheeses, barley bread and salted fish in silence.

A silence neither woman enjoyed.

Still irked, Juniper decided to focus on her questions and not her emotions. Putting the knife she was using down, "How would Uncle know you and Amias were connected and I didn't?"

"The birthmark."

"I've never seen a birthmark on you."

Anise lifted her long black hair off her neck, exposing the same crescent shaped birthmark.

Juniper's gently ran her fingers across it, but unlike Amias's, Anise's birthmark didn't shimmer under her touch.

"I don't understand."

"As you know, all of us are a descendant of a God or Goddess. Some may be blessed with their abilities. Most in modern day are not. The industrial revolution, among other things, became more important, and the memory and wisdom of the Gods faded away or died. Few remain. That is our quest. To help them remember." Tapping her finger to her own head and then on Juniper's.

Continuing, while finishing to prepare their lunch. "I am a direct descendant of the Goddess Artemis. Only those that carry her crescent moon hold her power. Rhen knew I held the birthmark, when he saw it on Amias's neck, he wasn't surprised."

"That still doesn't explain why when I touch your birthmark nothing happens, but when I touch Amias's birthmark, it comes to life and shimmers."

Anise stopped mid task. Did she hear her correctly? "His birthmark does what?"

"It glimmers."

"What else? What else has happened between the two of you?"

Juniper turned her face. It wasn't that she was ashamed, she just felt speaking about their intimacy was an invasion of their privacy and disrespectful to Amias.

Anise placed her hand on Juniper's chin, forcing her to look in her direction.

"Tell me."

"He doesn't become charred when we are intimate. I can actually let go without fear. My gifts are no longer a curse to my own sensuality with him."

The tone of Juniper's words changed to excitement. "He absorbed my currents. For instance, there was a moment when we first met that I was having a hard time controlling what my emotions had caused. The storm was becoming too much to handle and he instinctively knew what to do, he settled the storm that had been raging inside me. Which inturn, calmed the skies?"

Juniper watched as a large smile spread across Anise's face, her eyes filled with joy. "I should have known. He is your balance."

With tray in hand, Anise took a deep breath and headed back into the room where Rhen and her son were patiently waiting. Waiting for answers to questions she wasn't sure she had.

In the midst of their conversation neither Juniper, nor Anise, heard the door shut. So when they only found Rhen deep into his books and smoking his pipe and Amias nowhere to be seen, both women felt trepidation.

"Uncle, where is Amias?"

"He said he needed fresh air." Giving Anise a stern look, "Seems his head is filled with more than a demi-god should have to handle at once."

"Oh zip it! You knew exactly what I had to do and how it had to be done."

Rhen popped a piece of cheese into his mouth. "So you say."

Juniper was now frantically pulling on her cloak.

"Do you know what direction he went?"

Another piece of cheese. "What's the rush? Can't a man try and find some quiet from all the screaming in his head?" Shooting another stern look at Anise.

"Stop being so theatrical with your facial expressions Rhen, and tell Juniper where she can find my son."

"Son, huh? Have you even thought about how this is affecting him right now? His mother, whom he thought was dead, is actually alive and well. His half-brother is sitting on a throne that was supposed to be his, yet he was cast as a murderer of his father instead of the God he is!"

Rhen was now pacing the floor with hard footsteps, his hands flailing as he spoke in emphasising each word firmly.

"AND! AND! He was a guardian of a twin that can send this entire world upside down."

"I did what I had to do!" Anise shouted back

"Well you screwed up woman!"

"I didn't know Keelen would be the one sitting on the throne! It was supposed to be Amias."

The food must have hit his belly because Juniper could see Rhen's demeanor soften as he took his favorite chair.

"I'm sorry Anise. I shouldn't have raised my voice. I know you did what you thought was best."

Anise leaned back into the other overstuffed chair, resting her head against a blanket that was thrown over the top.

"It obviously didn't work completely because the omens have been delivered and we need to devise a plan."

The cat, who had been puzzled by the ebb and flow of voices, had now jumped into Anise's lap, purring in hopes to equalize the vibrations running through her.

Juniper shifted her feet. "So what's the plan?"

Rhen and Juniper both looked at Anise for direction.

"I'm thinking I need to see Isleen and Lady Una. They should have some insight on what's going on in the realm."

"Why don't we just go straight to the realm?" Juniper asked.

"WE aren't stepping foot in the lion's den until we know what we are up against."

"UGH!!!! I'm going to find Amias. And when I return with him, you best have a plan."

Juniper slammed the door with a mission.

~ Chapter 11 ~

The array of emotions were almost stifling. His entire life he blamed himself and the Gods for the death of his mother. That somehow he was unworthy of a mother's love.

She had loved him. Through her touch, he was able to feel her broken heart.

Amias stood on the rocks that jutted out into the sea. The waves crashed and the cold air licked at his tears.

Whenever he needed to think or decompress, the sea would call to him, calming what he could not control. What a fucking mess.

Every now and again a whiff of oil and an unnatural decay filled his nostrils. Will anything he and the others do be all for naught? Had man become so blinded by shiny objects, dirty money, and power, that they couldn't see the direct connection to the environment's health and the fertility of their future?

Flashes of her story persisted and he pushed them away, only to be jostled by images of Juniper. Oh Juniper, what should I do? He questioned himself.

Even with all this new information, the only time he had ever felt wanted, needed, or a King, was when she had given him permission to be hers. Juniper had become his true realm, and if she would allow him, he'd like to stay. But could he?

Clouds began rolling in and with it, the clapping thunder. Distracted in her search for Amias, Juniper hadn't noticed the change her emotions were causing. All she could think about was him and what he must be going through. Not that her head still wasn't spinning, but she was far from fragile. She had the blood of the Gods Boreaus and Njord running through her veins. She was as strong as the North wind and as powerful as the sea, and nothing and no one was going to stand in the way of her heart and her mission of her people.

Juniper spotted him and watched as he skimmed one last stone along the waves before turning and walking in her direction.
With her hands in her cloak she waited in anticipation. The wind began to dance wildly, picking up and lifting her long locks. And a raven's caw could be heard in the distance.
He didn't wait for her to speak. Amias had a gut feeling that this may be the last chance he would have her all to himself. The Gods had set their plan into motion, escaping it would be mute, but for now, in this moment, all he could think about was her and how she made him feel. Reaching her, Amias pulled her close, kissing her deeply. An electrical current shot through him as their tongues met, stirring his desire. Could she feel it? Could she feel his heart sing when she was wrapped up in his arms? Did she know that she had become so much more than a pawn in this game of the Gods?
As if on cue, Juniper pulled back, "If all goes awry and we fade, I want it to be in your arms."

Before he could respond Juniper reached down and pulled a piece of driftwood from the snow and began drawing a large circle around them. When she had finished and returned to the center, Amias watched Juniper close her eyes, hold her arms up to the roaring sky, and summon a ring of fire.

The snow quickly changed to sand.

Kissing the palm of his hand, "I don't want to think about what might be, or what is to come. All I want is you...right now...right here. The Gods be damned."

That's all he needed to hear. For once, he wasn't performing a duty for the Gods, or Vardon, or Keelen. He wasn't a guardian. Amias was just a man and he was hers.

Sliding his hand in her hair, Amias pulled her face to his so he could suck on her bottom lip, licking its sweetness. A low moan escaped him when his other hand squeezed her breasts, rolling her hard nipples between his finger and thumb.

He had to have her soon, time was running out and the bulge in his pants was starting to painfully throb.

Tugging her hair back so he could look into those beautiful violet eyes, "Do I have your permission?"

"Do with me what you will."

"Be careful what you say...I might not stop."

Amias got a glimmer of her sly smile just before she dropped to her knees, pulling out his hard cock and hungrily taking its entirety into her mouth. The talent of her tongue and fingers drove him crazy, as she worked a perfect suction. The vibration of her humming while sucking would surely bring him to his peak if she didn't slow down, and as much as he wanted to release, the desire to be deep inside her was stronger.

"Goddess...I won't be able to last if you continue."

One last suck... a lick on the tip of his throbbing head, "I am not a Goddess."

Technically she was a demi-goddess but he decided it was best to undress her than it was to correct her.

Inside the protective circle their desperation to cling to the moment was met with a heavy winter rain, squashing the fire.

Dark clouds rolled with thunder vibrating the sand beneath them, enhancing their already vibrating bodies.

Juniper had lost all sense of time and responsibility. All she knew was then and now. How wonderful it felt to have him inside her. To feel his hardness, to know it was safe for her to release the energy of the skies and the seas that boiled through her.

He was the balance that absorbed and calmed her. He was her touch stone.

Wrapping her legs around his waist, using her heels to push him deeper, Juniper could feel her core begin to quiver and tighten.

A moan of ecstasy escaped him when her back arched. Amias lifted his head to watch the warmth flush her cheeks and the rain puddled between them.

A normal person would have gone into hypothermia. But they were far from normal and he liked it that way.

Their bodies continued to move in rhythm, another crash from the heavens.

And, like a Mozart's emotionally charged piano concerto, lightning struck again and again, deafening their screams of passion while creating a castle of fulgurite, protecting them from the cawing of the crow.

If only the circle of petrified lighting could keep them safe, Amias thought to himself as he buttoned up his coat.

"You certainly know how to make a statement."

Running her finger up his chest. "Yeah, I've been known to do that every now and again."

"Oh, so you're famous now?"

"Why yes, haven't you heard? I char men with my fiery lady bits."

"You do have a habit of setting me on fire." Amias winks.

Juniper wrinkled up her nose, "Was that your attempt at being funny?"

"Didn't work?"

"Come on jester, let's get back to my uncle's before they start searching for us. We can work on your stand-up later."

****

"You two certainly put on a hell of a show." Rhen poured himself some mead. He knew Amias needed some time to put things right in his head but his niece knew better. Time was ticking.

"I did it just for you Uncle. Wouldn't want you to get bored while waiting."

Rhen grunted.

Ignoring her uncle's displeasure, Juniper kissed Anise on the cheek. "What have you been up to while I was creating a ruckus with the weather?" Another jab.

"I've been scrying."

"And?"

"I wasn't able to see Rowan. It was dark and I could smell decay." Amias pulled out the shattered talisman. With questioning eyes, he placed it in Anise's hand.

"This is not good. Was this yours?"

"No." Juniper interjected. "It was one of mine. I'm not sure if it happened before or after my dream, but if you add those two omens to the crow's gift of the twig then something disastrous is in motion."

"I agree."

Anise paused to pick up the cat that had been pacing a figure eight through her legs. "And since I can't seem to sense Rowan, we are going to have to see the next best thing...your mother."

"WHAT?" Juniper was taken aback. She had always wondered what it would be like to meet her mother, to search her face for a resemblance, to ask her if she regretted sending her here. Did she miss her? Could she sense what she had been going through? She knew she should be worrying about the fate of mankind and the obstacles that were standing in the way, but all she could feel was giddiness at the idea of a mother. Her mother.

"I suggest you get some sleep." Pointing a stern finger at Amias, "And I mean sleep."

****

Amias laid on his side, with his head propped up on his hand, watching as Juniper tossed and turned.

Opening one eye. "How long have you been staring at me?"

Moving the hair from her face, revealing her delicate features, "Half the night. You have quite a left hook."

"I hit you? Oh my Goddess I'm so sorry."

Amias licked his lips, "It's okay, I've felt worse. Bad dreams?"

"Not bad. I just have all these questions buzzing through my head. I can't seem to quiet myself."

"Can I help?"

"What's it like?"

"What is what like?"

"The modern world. I've read a dozen books but to actually experience it…"

"I don't think we will be there long enough for you to take it all in."

"True, but I'm very curious."

Rolling her over on top of him. "Curiosity killed the cat."

A quick peck on his lips. "Satisfaction brought it back."

"Let me do the satisfying."

"Do I hear jealousy in your tone?"

"Perhaps."

"Well don't be…I just want to experience what my sister already has."

"I'll see what I can do." Flipping her back over before sitting up. "If we don't start getting ready I may never let you leave this bed."

"Maybe a little quickie?"

"Nothing with you is quick."

Juniper didn't really want a quickie, she knew the only reason she mentioned it was to borrow some time. Hating to admit it, she was scared. Scared that her mother wouldn't be what she had imagined, that she, herself, wouldn't be what her mother expected her to be. All this uncertainty was making her anxious.

Amias wrapped a scarf around Juniper, kissing the tip of her nose.

"You look like you're about to puke."

"Is it that obvious?"

"That you're petrified? Yes."

"Quickie?"

Amias laughed, "Nice try."

In unison, they took a deep breath and headed out into a nautical twilight. Neither knowing if they would return to the safety of the lighthouse together.

Unbeknownst to Juniper, a small box with a lovers knot, carved in Amias's hand and adorn with pink and white seashells, lay on the sill.

And when the first rays of sun break through the tower's windows, a sailor's valentine waits, holding his heart.

~ Chapter 12 ~

Standing on the pier, Anise and Rhen waited. Her heart pounding in competition with the waves. Juniper thought it would rip right through her chest.

"So how does this work?"

"I sent word last night. Everything is ready at the other end, so it will be quick," Anise replied.

"I don't understand. Don't we need to summon the veil?"

"Not for this. In a few moments there will be ripe between the "now", and we will step through it."

Amias took Juniper's trembling hand, "Our world is parallel to the one your mother is in. But you're right, we will need to summon a veil to return to the realm."

Reaching out, Anise took Juniper's other hand, while Rhen took hers and Amias.

The rising sun, casting a shadow on the circle of four, burst into sparkes of amber as they stood against the force of the North wind only to be warmed by the South.

"Open your eyes." Amias leaned in and kissed the side of Juniper's head and whispered, "My love, could you loosen your grip? You're going to break my hand."

Juniper slowly released his hand and opened her eyes.

In front of them blanketed in Carolina jasmine, stood a house. Their sweet scent was almost as breathtaking as their butter-yellow blossoms. But not as breathtaking as the woman standing on the front porch. Her long dark hair was secured back with what looked like paint brushes. She wore a floral slip dress and an apron. Juniper caught a whiff of linseed oil.

"Is that food I smell?" Rhen asked Isleen as he climbed the steps with the help of his staff.

"Really?" Anise shook her head. Following him up the steps, "Ignore him...all he can think about lately is food. Trust me, he is far from starving."

Isleen smiled. "Nice to see you Anise. You look well."

"Wish it was under better circumstances, and thank you, I am doing well for an old lady."

Isleen nodded at Amias, then focused her attention on Juniper.

"This isn't how I thought we would reunite. I wanted it to be less drastic and more fluid."

Juniper's eyes met her mother's for the first time. A faucet of emotions began to pour out. All she had been feeling throughout her life, the years of pushing them down, were now traveling down her face and onto her mother's shoulder as she held her, stroking her auburn hair, allowing her own tears to fall.

"Ehem," Rhen piped in. "Not to ruin this reunited mushy moment, but we really need to start planning our next move."

"You really have no couth." Anise whispered under her breath.

"What? Am I wrong?"

"I don't know why I even brought you along."

"You brought me because I, and I alone, can handle my brother, Vardon."

"Oh just wipe that self-satisfying grin off your face before I turn you into a newt."

The porch filled with laughter and the Bleeding Hearts and Bougainvillea laughed with them in the warm southern breeze.

****

The three of them may have been speaking, but Juniper was off in another world, literally. The glow of the lamp and the scent of patchouli mixed with lavender and linseed made her feel sleepy. Every now and again she would catch the twinkling of the colored lights on the evergreen that stood on the other side of the room. She wondered what it would be like to celebrate Saturnalia with her mother, would they combine it with her modern world Christmas. Is this new adventure part of the God's plan? Does meeting her mother signify spring...a new beginning? It was all exhausting.

Isleen recognized that faraway look on Juniper's face. She had seen it many times on Rowan.

"Juniper honey, are you okay?"

"Hmmm?"

"You seem distracted and you have barely eaten a thing?"

"I'm good...really. I'm just not very hungry."

Amias leaned back in his chair, stretching his arms out then laying one around Juniper.

"Well I can't get enough. This is really good." Rhen was on his second helping of chili only nodding and grunting in between bites.

"You are such a glutton. Here." Anise handed him a napkin. "Wipe your beard."

"I see Anise is still as bossy as ever."

All heads turned in the direction of the woman speaking.

"At least I know how to take charge, unlike you, Lady Una."

"Nice gray. I see your age has finally started to set in."

"Not as quickly as yours."

Before the bickering could continue, Rhen jumped in, "Ladies, could you please set aside your issues? We need to focus on the issue at hand, not past pettiness. Plus, this isn't how Juniper should meet her grandmother."

Under her breath, yet loud enough for Lady Una to hear, Anise had the last word, "Yeah, your very great, great, great, then add some more greats, grandmother."

"Really Anise?" Lady Una murmured back.

Juniper was finding the banter between the two women quite comical. How curious they were. For two very old and wise women, they sure knew how to act like children. Whoever said people mellowed with age certainly hadn't been in the same room with these two and Juniper hoped it would never change. This, she thought, this was family.

Lady Una noticed Juniper's amusement.

"Ignore us old bats and come here."

Juniper walked into Lady Una's open arms and for the first time she knew what it felt like to be hugged tightly by a grandmother. No matter how many "greats" were attached, it filled her with joy.

Lady Una released her and stepped back so she could look into Juniper's eyes, "Shall we try and figure this all out together? I hear you are quite talented when it comes to maneuvering the four elements."

"Of course she is," Anise piped in. "She has had me as her teacher."

Lady Una rolled her eyes and flashed a quick wink before joining the rest of them at the table.

Juniper began by telling Lady Una about her dream and the gift from the raven, the broken talisman and how the weather was getting harder to control. She didn't need to mention how Amias's crescent birthmark responded to her touch. She already knew.

Anise to Lady Una. "Why can't I see Rowan when I scrye? I can sense her but it's not easy."

"Nothing is going as the Gods had planned. Vardon has gone back on his word, just like you predicted. I had hoped with the union of Keelen and Rowan, we could have avoided this. Rowan's gifts are strong but she is naive when it comes to spotting a wolf. She should have been warned about her father's plan."

Anise leaned forward, placing her hands on either side of her tea. "That mistake lands on you."

"Maybe had you not left, then your son would be sitting in his rightful place and I wouldn't have had to make do with what you left me with." Lady Una reminded.

"Do you really want to go there?" Anise spat.

Juniper sat with a large smile on her face. Amias could tell she was really enjoying the banter. He loved the way her eyes lit up when her curiosity peaked. She must have been one mischievous child. He wished he would have known her then.

Turning his attention to the two squabbling women, "Ladies, it doesn't matter who did or didn't do certain things. What does matter is the now."

Rhen savoured the last bite of his cherry tart, "The boy's right. The two of you are giving me a headache."

Amias touched the top of Lady Una's hand. "Where is Rowan?"

"I don't know," she whispered. Tears began to well as she continued. "Everything was going swimmingly, but then Vardon sent Keelen on some made-up mission, and while he was gone, Rowan disappeared."

Isleen stared out the window. The palm trees swayed to an unheard waltz. She heard the words, but she couldn't digest them. "I can still feel her. The bastard has her hidden."

Rhen, stroking his beard, "Makes sense. If one hides the truth then the lies become the truth. With her out of the way, he can carry out his mission."

Leaning into Juniper's ear, Amias secretly ran his tongue along its edge, whispering, "You want to escape this pow-wow and have some fun?"

That's all Juniper needed to hear.

Injecting herself into the conversation, "Excuse me. May I speak? I realize that we have some serious work ahead of us, and that all outcomes need to be assessed, but the one thing you haven't considered is….me. Vardon has no idea I exist and when we find Rowan, and we will find her. Have any of you thought about the power the two of us will have when we are joined?" Juniper took one deep cleansing breath, exhaling her stress. "Now, I'm going to bid you all good-bye and go have some fun while I still can."

"Your sister would have said the same thing," Isleen responded. Then adding, "I would suggest a change of clothes. I'm sure your sister wouldn't mind. Amias knows the way."

~ Chapter 13 ~

The modern world was so much more than what she had read in books. In books it all seemed larger than life. Full of excitement and adventure. The land of the plenty, where prosperity was available to all.

But as Amias led Juniper along Ocean Dr., Juniper's rose-colored glasses faded. The once pastel colors of the buildings had faded, many of their windows covered with wood and graffiti. The hum of the electrical currents buzzing across the wired sky battled with the roar of airplanes, boats, and cars. Her nose burned from the toxins in the air.

With his hand on the base of her back, Amias led Juniper across a parking lot, passing several beach goers, and down a worn path, leading her to the beach. He was finding it hard not to "gift" her bare shoulder with love bites.

"You haven't said much since we left. Are you okay?"

"Just anxious to get to the ocean. I need to recharge."

"Recharge?"

"Remind me when this is all over to step up your lessons. Water in motion produces negative ions, and those ions give me energy and calm me at the same time. I do my best work when I'm in my element."

Amias gave Juniper the space she requested. Watching from a distance.

Removing her sister's sneakers and handing them to Amias, she drifted across the sand until she reached the water's edge.

Taking what the water offered, a sense of sadness washed over her. The water here was so much different. It had changed. And she could smell it and feel the shift in its depths. It was more vital now than ever to send a chain reaction out into the universe. And her hand alone was not enough.

Amias walked up behind her pulling her closer into his chest, resting his hands on the bare skin between her top and skirt. Her hair smelled of lotus and the sea and he buried his face deeper into her mane.

"It's just you and I...stop thinking babe."

"My heart just hurts so much. They have no idea the ramifications of their actions."

"No, they don't, but you and I and those we have sent out into the world...they will bring it all into light before more damage is done."

Turning to face him.

"How can you be so sure? According to the elders and from what you have told me, their fertility is dying along with mother earth."

He could see her searching for assurance in his face but he had none to give.

"I can't be a hundred percent sure, but I have faith. Faith in you."

Amias held her face, tracing his thumb across her parted lips. He could drown in her and never want for air.

"Oh my God! Rowan?!!!"

Amias turned to see Anna running towards them, leaving her friends behind.

"Who is that?" Juniper whispered

"Anna, one of your sister's friends...let me handle it."

Anna was out of breath but it didn't keep her from throwing her arms around her best friend and hugging her.

"When did you get back? When your mom told me you were off backpacking in Europe and with the Viking...I was like..Woah!"

Anna looked over at Amias, scrunching her nose, "Why is he here?" Looking around, "Where's your stud muffin?"

Quickly, Amias answered for her. "Rowan was just telling me that Keelen was still in Europe. We just bumped into each other on our way to the Kitchen Club."

"Well that's a downer."

"Are you heading back to the club?" Amias questioned.

"Gawd no. It's Pink Floyd night." Hugging Juniper one last time. "It really is so good to see you. I've missed you. Call me tomorrow?"

Juniper hugged her back. She never had a best friend. She was raised with a purpose, and that purpose didn't include late night pizza, movies, manicures and boys. She was to keep the human race from destroying itself and the earth that held them.

Juniper reluctantly released Anna. "Sure...tomorrow."

Anna, still holding her hands. "Rowan are you okay?"

A tear slipped through the cracks of Junipers walls. "I feel like I've been gone a lifetime."

"But you're back now Roe and we can spend this entire winter break catching up before I head back to college."

"Yeah…of course we can."

Anna joined her gaggle of friends and headed away from the Kitchen Club, but not before turning around and shouting, "Rowan girl, I love you!"

"I could love you too." Juniper whispered to herself as she watched the friend she never had disappear into a starry sky.

****

"Are you ready to get turned on by something other than me?" Amias shouted.

The band was playing their rendition of "Welcome to the Machine" as they squeezed their way through the haze of marijuana and nicotine, trying to reach the bar.

"Is that even possible?"

"In a way…yes."

Amias handed Juniper a Coors.

"What's this?"

"It's beer. Kinda like our ale."

"You know what alcohol does to me. Do you think this is wise considering what's to come in the morning?"

"Yes I do. And the only cumming we are going to be focused on is you and tonight…"

One can't argue with that she thought. Holding out her beer, "A toast to letting loose and cumming."

Juniper's amusement was suddenly broken when Amias, recognizing the change in tempo, immediately led her out onto the crowded dance floor. If she was going to feel anything tonight, it was going to be euphoric he thought.

Standing behind her, "I want you to lean back into me and close your eyes…and just feel the music..don't listen..feel."

Juniper closed her eyes and followed his instructions.

The piano, then the organ….softly the musicians began to play. A guitar. Between the beer and the contact buzz Juniper felt light. Her arms wrapped around Amias's neck, she began to sway to "The Great Gig in the Sky."

She wasn't sure if it was agony or acceptance she felt when the woman's voice echoed against the waves of notes, but whatever it was it stirred her core, causing a tingling sensation between her thighs. Tilting her head back she pulled his face towards hers, kissing him deeply as she continued to sway.

He should have immediately taken her off to some dark corner of the club, but the music and the mood had him grounded and while their tongues danced, Amias held on to her with his left hand and slipped his right down the top of her skirt.

Juniper pushed her back harder into his chest while tilting her hips, allowing him to dip his fingers deep inside her folds.

Faster…faster..his fingers darted..wetter and wetter she became and as the band reached the crescendo, Juniper released her own vocals into the mouth of her lover.

The band had switched to "Another Brick in the Wall" and Amias was now beyond turned on and he needed a dark corner.

Catching the glow of a neon exit sign, Amias pulled Juniper through it, pushing her up against the paint chipped wall. He didn't just want to have her, he wanted to devour and feed the never-ending hunger of her.

Just in case.

He could taste the salt air on her lips, her neck, and her delicate clavicle.

He tried feverishly to kiss away her fears, hoping to assure her she was not standing alone.

Amias gathered her skirt up around her waist allowing him to massage deeply her heart shaped ass while grinding his throbbing and eager cock between her thighs.

Instinctively, Juniper maneuvered out of her panties, giving him permission to play within her wetness. Tilting her hips, Juniper begged for penetration.

Tonight, her aching would only be soothed with the forceful thrusts of his passion.

And his only sanctuary would be within the tightness of her warm walls.

Amias, with one hand, held her wrists above her head never letting his lips falter from hers, and with his other hand, cradled and guided her hips into the glorious climax of "Eclipse" being played inside the Kitchen Club.

Consumed in their static, the heavens began creating their own.

Lightning flickered behind the dark clouds as a violent circulation of air swirled releasing a microburst of torrential rain, and like a sponge, Juniper with eyes wide opened, absorbed the God Taranis's offering.

Amias's attempt to shelter Juniper from the stinging rain failed.

Darting out from under his arm, she began twirling in the cloudburst reminding him of a dandelion floret gone to seed, blowing wishes to the Gods.

Ceasing as quickly as it started, the downpour stopped and the clouds broke free, dissipating into the starry night.

"Oh Amias wasn't that beautiful?!"

"You're beautiful."

"I could dance in the rain forever."

"I have no doubt you could, however forever is not now. We should probably head back to your mother's and change out of these soaked clothes."

Posing for him, "Don't you like the way I look?"

"You would look good in a puddle of mud." Taking her hand, "Let's grab some local food, my sweet water siren."

As they walked through Little Havana hand in hand, the aroma of black beans, chicken and flann made Juniper salvate. The faint sound of music could be heard coming from a portable radio where several men were gathered around a table playing dominoes, their cigars in hand.

On both sides of the street buildings were painted in hues of salmon and aqua. A stray dog ran down an alley.

Amias stopped in front of an outdoor cafe.

"I'll order our food."

Juniper smiled, continuing to watch the men play.

An older gentleman sat behind the counter.

In broken english, "What can I get you?"

"We will have two Cafe Con Leche and two Cubano's."

The old man nodded.

Amias leaned against the counter. "I like the culture here. The food is amazing, the music moody, and faith is in abundance."

Juniper never heard Amias speak so passionately about the modern world. This new depth of his personality made her wonder if he would choose to return here instead of returning to the island with her.

Amias continued with his thought, "Did you know that unlike most of America where the elderly are shipped off to nursing homes and forgotten, here they're remembered, respected and they never lose their purpose in life?"

Turning to face Juniper, "Just like our realm, the older one gets, the more important they become."

Juniper found his words endearing. "Well... they are the holders of the past and teachers for future generations."

"That's the thing...soon this culture will change too and they have no idea what they are throwing away."

Before their conversation could turn into a reminder of what the dawn would bring, the two of them, still soaking wet, headed on their way with food in hand and courage in their quiver.

~ **Chapter 14** ~

The house was quiet but for the crackling of the fire in the fireplace and the distant clanking of dishes in the kitchen.

"I'm going to head up to Rowan's room and get out of these wet clothes. Thank you for a wonderful night. I really did have fun."

"As did I."

Amias watched as Juniper climbed the staircase. It had been a good night. One he hoped to have more of.

"Well aren't you a sight."

Amias turned to see Lady Una.

"Ah yes, good evening Lady Una." Pausing to look down upon himself, "We got caught in the rain."

"I guess so, you're soaked to the bone. Best you get out of those clothes before you catch a chill. You will find your proper clothes laid out for you upstairs, last room at the end of the hall."

"Proper?"

"I thought it was best if you dressed in something that was inconspicuous. We have no idea who Vardon has working with him...no one needs to know you have returned to the realm. It will give us an upper hand."

"Thank you, I appreciate it."

"Go get a few winks, we will be leaving at dawn."

"Lady Una...I...I want to say I'm sorry. I know you must think I'll of me, and you have every right to be angry. I've done some terrible things, made bad decisions but you have to believe me when I say I have changed. Juniper has changed me. I'm not the man I once was."

"It is not I, you need forgiveness from. You need to regain the trust of your brother, Keelen, and Rowan. Your storm, the one raging inside you, I believe has turned direction. Now get to bed, the Gods are waiting for you to help set their plan in motion and you won't be any good if you're tired."

"You're right. Good night Lady Una"

"Good night."

Amias ascended the stairs leading Lady Una to tend to her twilight ritual.

****

The sun was just breaking when Juniper woke. Buried deep in pillows and blankets she watched the dust dance in the first rays of light. The sound of movement from downstairs was a reminder that time had run out and no matter how deep she burrowed herself she couldn't escape.

Isleen leaned inside the door frame. "Hey sleepy head."

"Hey." Juniper sat up rubbing the sleep from her eyes.

"Do you mind if I sit? I'd like to have a quick chat before you and the others start out."

"Only if it means I can stay in this comfy bed longer?"

"Didn't you sleep well?"

"Not really...same dream...same omen. Same raven."

"I can't make those go away, only you can do that. As for our conversation, I'll do my best to drag it out."

Isleen sat on the edge of the bed, brushing the hair back from Juniper's face.

"I want to apologize. I have been so involved charting out our plan that we haven't had a quiet moment to get to know one another."

"It's okay. I'm used to it. All part of the role I've been chosen to play."

"My sweet girl, you are so much more than a "role" and it's not okay to be comfortable with that."

"Oh I know. I'm not complaining. I like having the gifts that I have, matter of fact, I want to be able to do more. I mean...yeah...it gets a little lonely at times but I would never change my life for a different one." Wiggling her fingers in front of her face. "You'd be amazed at what these two small hands are capable of conjuring."

Isleen smiled, nodding in agreement. Her daughters may look alike but their personalities were definitely on different ends of the spectrum. Juniper exuded confidence. She owned her strengths and weaknesses, uncertainty of who she will become wasn't in her vocabulary.

"You know what old man, I'm going to poison your next meal if you don't stop nagging me about food!" Anise yelled down to Rhen while climbing up the stairs.

"You're a bitter woman!" he shouted back.

"Better to be bitter than an old washed up God!"

Juniper and Isleen broke out in laughter when Anise entered the room carrying an armful of clothes.

"That man is on my last nerve."

Anise draped the dress she was holding over the oriental dressing screen.

"Juniper, I hope you don't mind but I took the privilege of picking you out a gown that was more fitting than what you usually wear."

"Not at all. I love the color." Walking behind the screen. "We really are going to do this, aren't we mother?"

"Are you doubting yourself?"

"Hardley. I feel like the war goddess, Brigid, on her way to battle." Coming out from behind the screen. "I've been pondering what kind of death Vardon will have."

"That's up to the Gods, not you," Anise flatly replied.

"Is it?"

Lady Una peered into the room, "If you three don't hurry up there is going to be a battle downstairs in the kitchen. That man is insufferable when he hasn't been fed."

"If we didn't have to leave soon I would make him suffer." responded Anise.

"Be nice you two. He may be grouchy but he is my uncle and I find him amusing."

The three women took their leave, but not before Isleen took a moment to turn on Rowans radio. "I thought you could use a little music to dress by."

****

Amias paced. No matter how many lists of pro's and con's he ran through his head, he always came up with the same answer and he didn't like it. It would be so much easier if mankind would just open their eyes to what they were doing instead of being selfish.

At least Rhen had stopped complaining and was now busy feeding his face.

"You pace a lot." Rhen finished his coffee. "Amias, you can't go into this second guessing yourself. If you do, you shall surely fail."

Amias stopped. "I'm not, I...just...I just don't know if I want the same things I used to."

"Ahhh, you've got a bit of a conundrum."

"Oh look the bear has finally stopped growling," Anise pointed out as they joined them in the kitchen.

"With no help from you. Are we ready?"

"I believe so. Just waiting on Juniper."

Directing his words to Amias, "Take note, you will spend the rest of your life waiting on a woman."

"If that woman is Juniper, it will be well worth it."

"Smart answer my boy, smart answer."

****

        Sitting on the edge of the bed Juniper had just finished lacing up her boots when Amias appeared.

"How long have you been out there in the hallway?"

"Long enough to get a peek at those lovely knees."

"I see Lady Una dressed you too. You look very handsome."

Amias knelt down in front of her, bringing her hands to his lips, placing a kiss upon each.

"What is it? And don't try and tell me nothing because your face is giving you away."

"What if I asked you to run away with me? We could go to another realm or return to the island."

Pulling her hands away. "I can't believe you are even suggesting it. No..No..I'm going through the veil. I'm finding my sister, I'm going to shock the hell out of Vardon and I'm going to make things right with the Gods. Why would you say that?"

"I'm sorry I brought it up. I know what we have to do but have you ever just wanted to not do what was expected of you?" To just follow your heart?"

"I don't run away from my responsibilities. How would you feel if you were my sister? She's in an entirely new world, her husband has been sent off and her new found father has hidden her away somewhere, or even worse. And my heart...my heart is to my Gods and Goddesses."

"I'm sorry...I wasn't thinking beyond us."

"Obviously."

"This was not how I planned to spend the last few moments alone."

Amias pushed back Juniper's red velvet gown, exposing her knees and began placing feathery kisses on them, his fingers sinking into her thighs.

Looking up at her. "I'm afraid."

Amias kisses moved farther up Junipers thighs. "I'm afraid I'll lose you."

His mouth now on the fabric covering her. "I couldn't endure the pain that would cause me."

Juniper knew she should be listening to what he was saying but all her body was listening to was the sensations his kisses were causing. So she parted her thighs. If she was going off to battle, she deserved this. Amias took his time bringing her to orgasm and when he was done and could no longer hold his own tethered desire, he made love to her like he would lose her.

And Juniper heard the Ravens caw.

I will continue to care for the arbor of our love.

I will tend to our fleecened flocks.

And memorize the sweet songs of small birds

And night violinists.

Until you come home...

To me.

Book 3
Coming soon